This Book

Belongs To

____